a note to parents

Little Owl Fun-time Readers are a delightful series of rhymes which have been specially written to be enjoyed by younger children.

Read the rhymes out loud to your child at first, so that he or she can learn the rhythm of the words. Perhaps later you could encourage your child to read them for him or herself or maybe even to memorize some of the shorter rhymes.

The Sleepy Monster
and other stories

poems by Clive Hopwood

illustrated by Heather Clarke,
Paul Crompton and Jean White

My Favourite Little Monster

There's a monster in my bedroom.
He lives beneath my bed.
He is my favourite monster –
and I call him Snuggly Fred.
He's the friendliest of monsters.
He's funny and he's kind.
But when I want to hug him
he is very hard to find!

My mummy doesn't like him.
She says he should be good.
He shouldn't ever tease the cat
or fill her shoes with mud.
My daddy is quite frightened
by my monster's roars.
But . . . my monster's just as frightened
when he hears my daddy's snores!

I love my little monster.
He's really good as gold.
It isn't ever his fault
that he won't do as he's told.
He hates to wash behind his ears.
He likes to stay up late.
My mummy says he's naughty –
but I think that he's great!

Dennis the Dinosaur

Dennis was a dinosaur
who danced the whole day long,
and as he danced he liked to sing,
and so he sang this song . . .

Oh, Dennis was a dinosaur . . .

The Sleepy Monster

I am a monster
from the deep.
When I'm awake
I'm not asleep.
When I'm asleep
I always dream
of swimming in
a shallow stream.

Monster Happiness

He was hairy.
He was tall.
He was much bigger
than us all.
He was handy
in a storm:
he'd cuddle up
and keep us warm.

Look Out for Dragons

Once upon a long ago
there were dragons, as you know.
They were friendly, good as gold,
people loved them, so I'm told.
Now they're gone, that lovely sight,
but if you look outside at night,
as the sunset fills the sky
you'll see dragons flying high.

How to Look After Your Monster

Make sure you feed him every day –
you don't want him to run away.
Keep him warm and dry at night.
Teach him not to chew or bite.
Show him how to dance and sing.
Always tell him everything.
Be kind and thoughtful to the end
and he will be your lifelong friend.

Stinkypoo

Down in the slime
where the sludgebogs stew
lives a monster,
Stinkypoo.
Muddy, murky
is his lair –
but I hear
he likes it there.

The Monster Sale

There was a monster sale last week –
I really wanted one –
but they must have sold them all,
for every one was gone.
But then I saw behind some crates
a monster oh so sad.
So I emptied out my purse
to see how much I had.

"That's just enough," the man told me.
"The price is very cheap,
because it is so horrible,"
which made the monster weep.
"Would you like it wrapped?" he asked,
but I answered, "No."
I took the monster by its claw
and said, "It's time to go."

Hand in claw we walked along,
strolling side by side.
When people saw us they all screamed
and ran away to hide.
I don't care what people say,
I think it looks just fine.
(And I know that secretly
they'd like a friend like mine!)